DREAM DOODLE DRAW!
Dress-Up Time

By Sonali Fry
Illustrated by Valeria Valenza

LITTLE SIMON

New York London Toronto Sydney New Delhi

The doodles in this book were created by

_____

LITTLE SIMON

An imprint of Simon & Schuster Children's Publishing Division

1230 Avenue of the Americas, New York, New York 10020

First Little Simon paperback edition April 2015

Copyright © 2015 by Simon & Schuster, Inc.

For information about special discounts for bulk purchases,

please contact Simon & Schuster Special Sales at 1-866-506-1949 or business@simonandschuster.com.

Manufactured in China 0215 SCP

2   4   6   8   10   9   7   5   3   1

ISBN 978-1-4814-2556-8

Get ready to play dress-up!

These girls are getting ready for a tea party.

Color in their fancy clothes!

These ladies are looking for necklaces
to wear with their ball gowns.
Can you doodle some around their necks?

These kids want to try on cool glasses.
Draw them in!

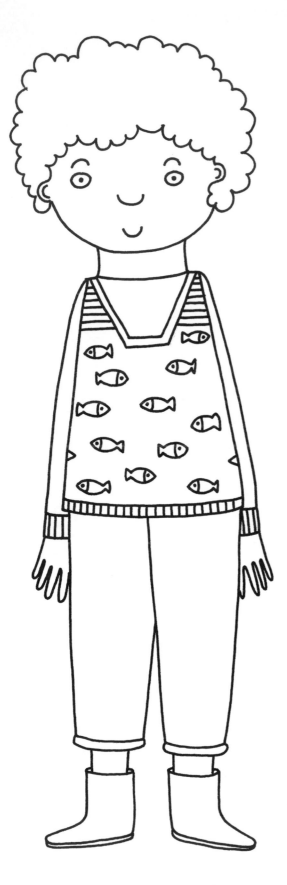

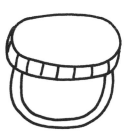

This superhero needs a cape!
Can you pick one for him? Color it in!

Trace the dotted lines to complete this tea set!

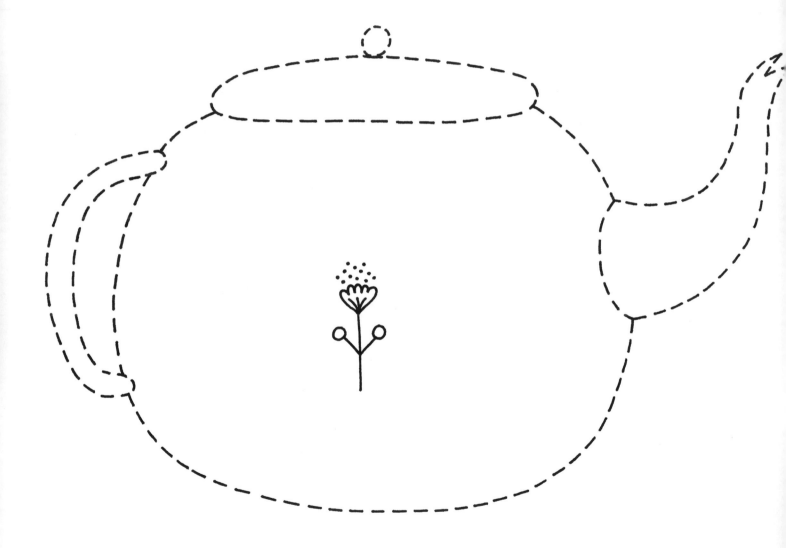

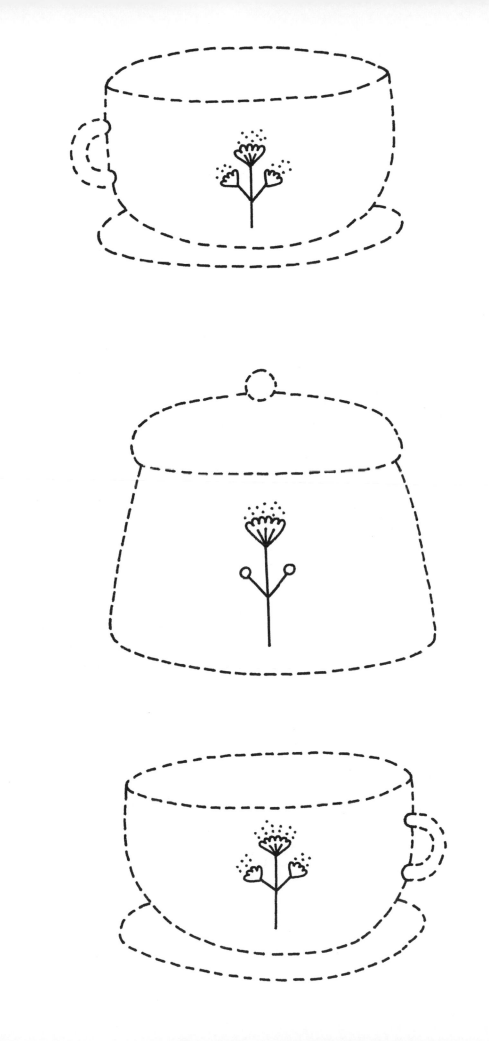

These fairies need wands!

Can you draw some for them?

Look at the two scenes on these pages.
Can you spot the eight differences? Circle them!

Look at all these clothes! If you were going to a fancy dinner party, what would you wear?
Circle the items, and then color them in!

If you could design your own dress, what would it look like?
Draw it for everyone to see!

Now draw a pair of shoes to go with it!

Trace the dotted lines to complete these great outfits!

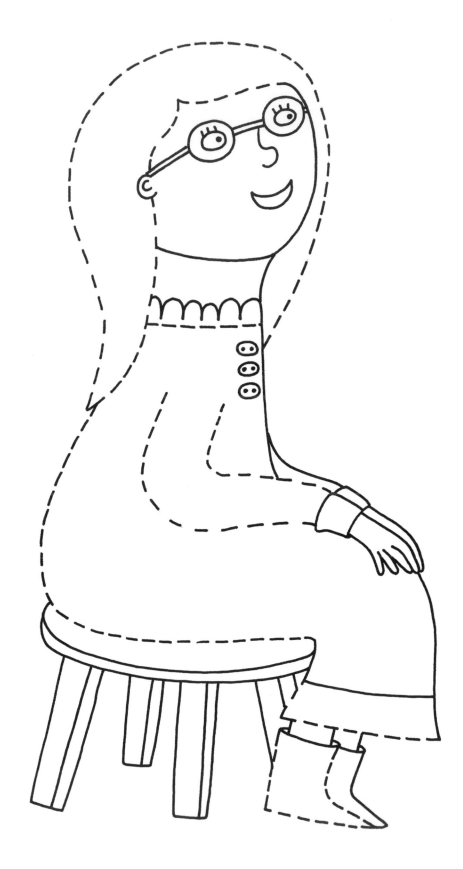

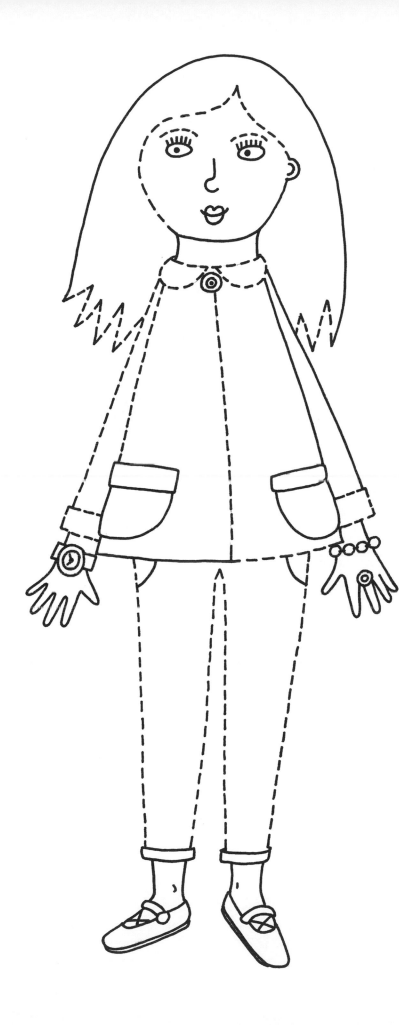

Look at all these beautiful bracelets!
Can you find the two that are exactly alike? Circle them!

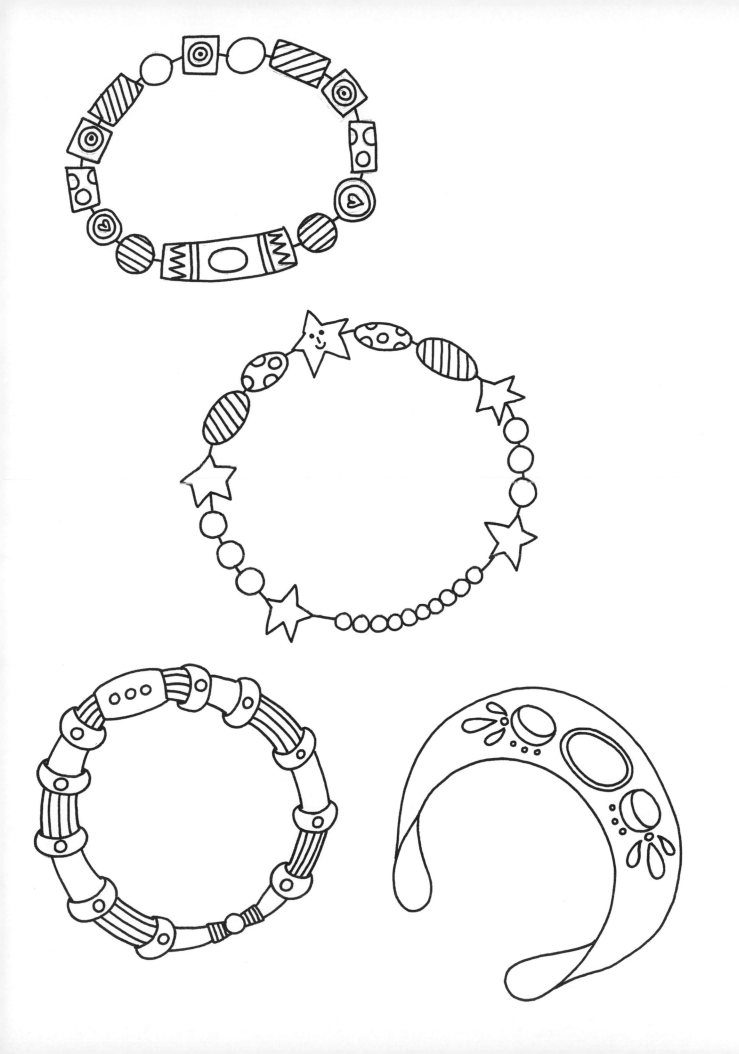

Draw some fun feather boas around these ladies' necks!

Two of these gentlemen are missing their moustaches.
Draw them in!

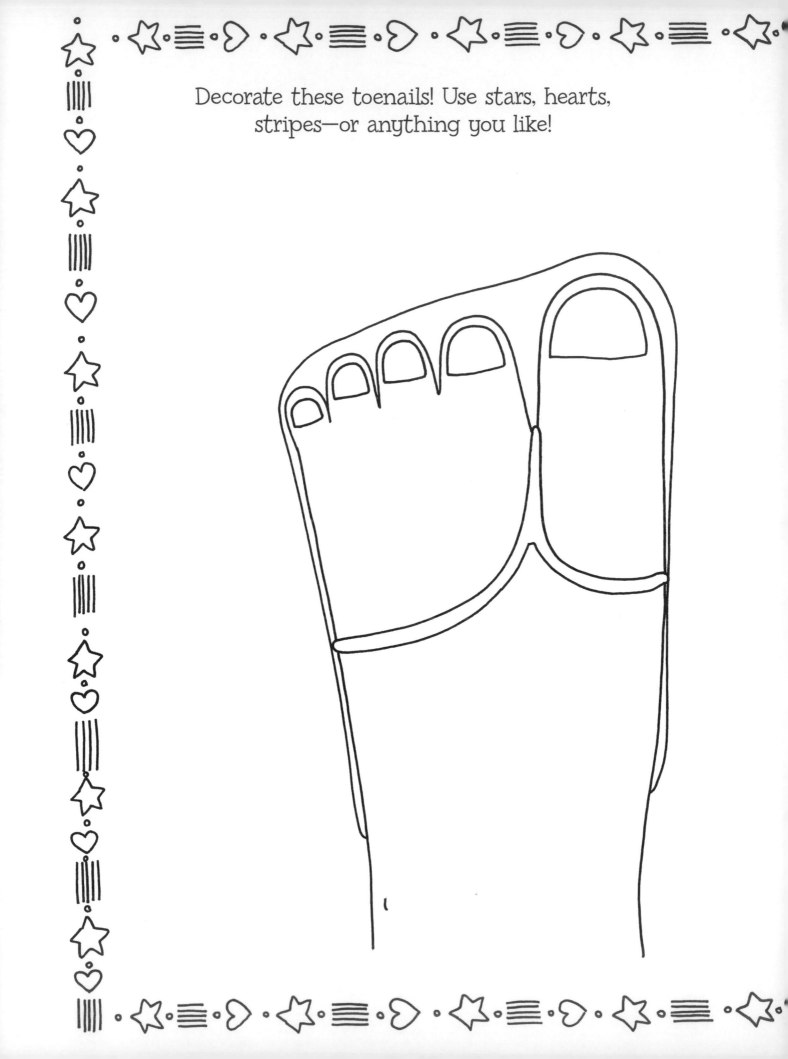

Decorate these toenails! Use stars, hearts,
stripes—or anything you like!

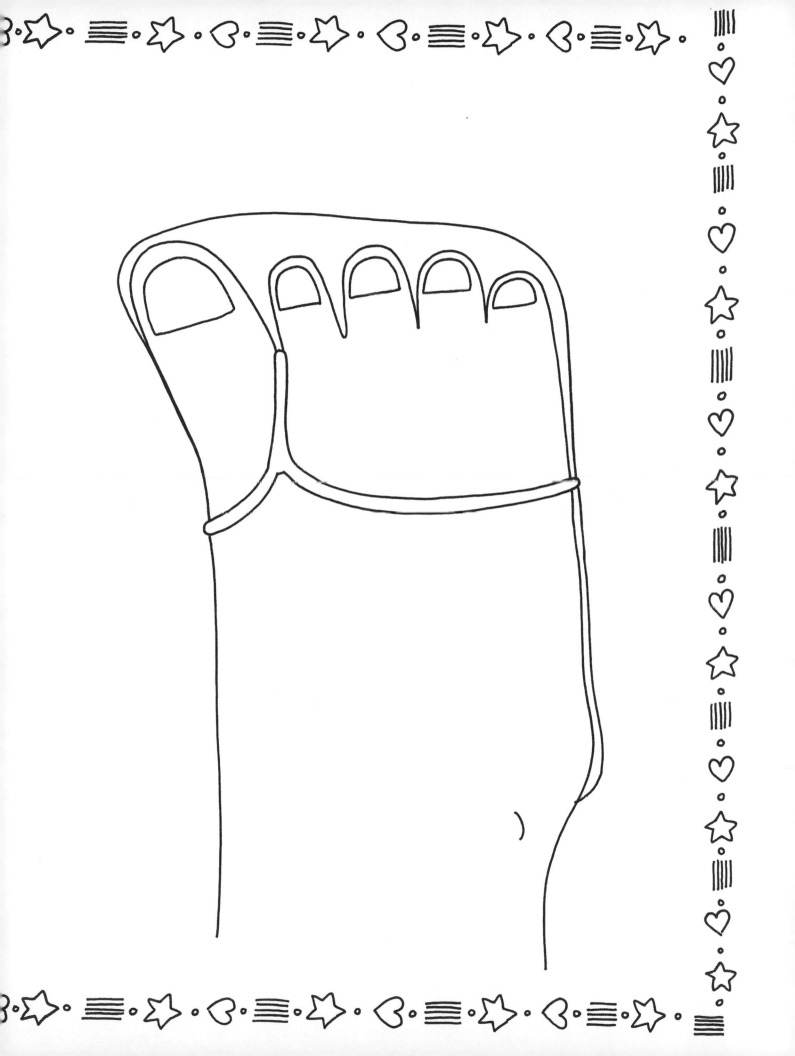

Decorate these dresses any way you like!

Add some unique hair styles to these people!

There are five crowns hidden in this scene.
Can you find them?
Color them in!

These men need bow ties. Doodle some in!

Can you put the finishing touches on this scene?
Hint: Add in pirate hats, eye patches, and swords.

Now color in the scene!

Oh no! It's raining!
Add some umbrellas to the scene to keep the bumblebee
and ladybug dry.

Color in these scarves!

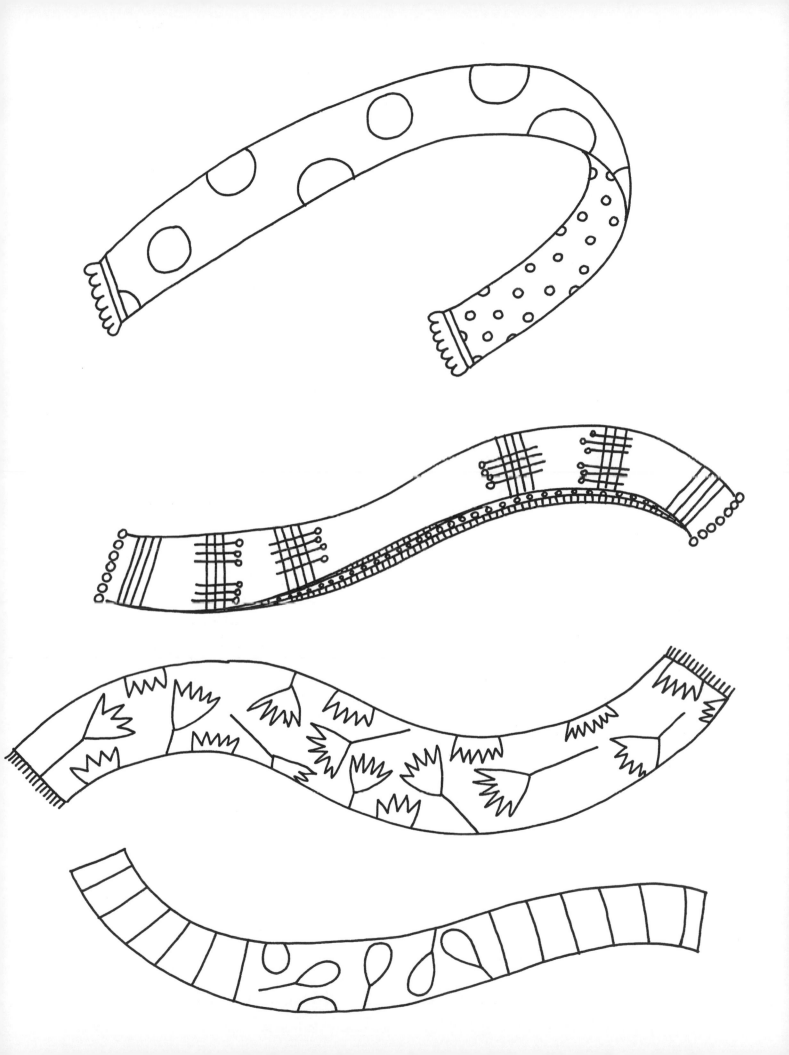

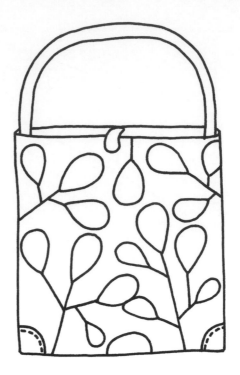

Which bag is your favorite? Color it in!

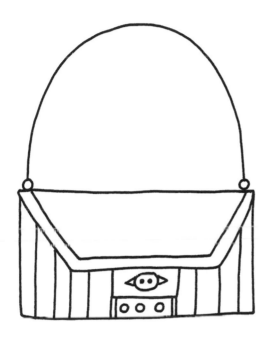

Now color in the rest!

Connect the dots to create some stockings.

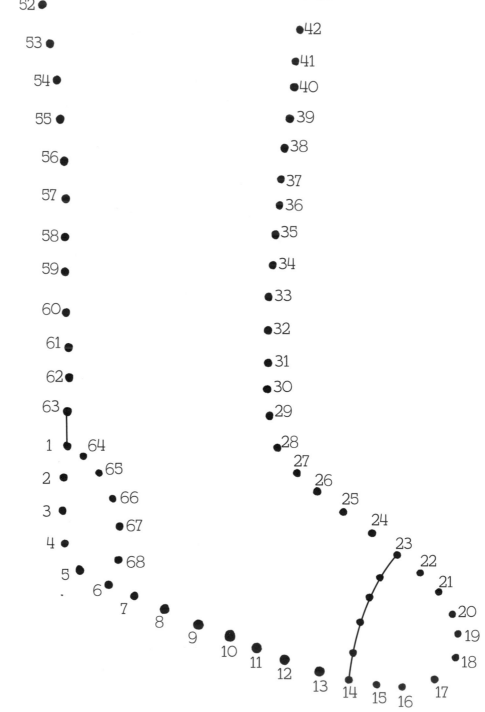

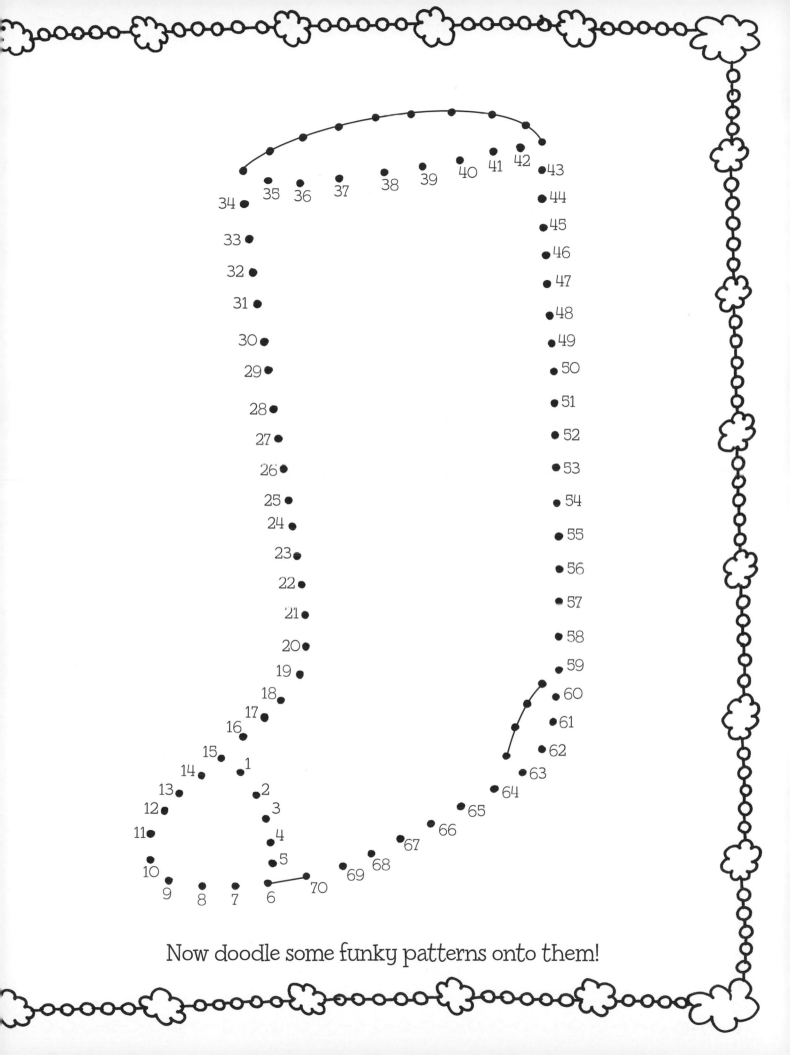

Now doodle some funky patterns onto them!

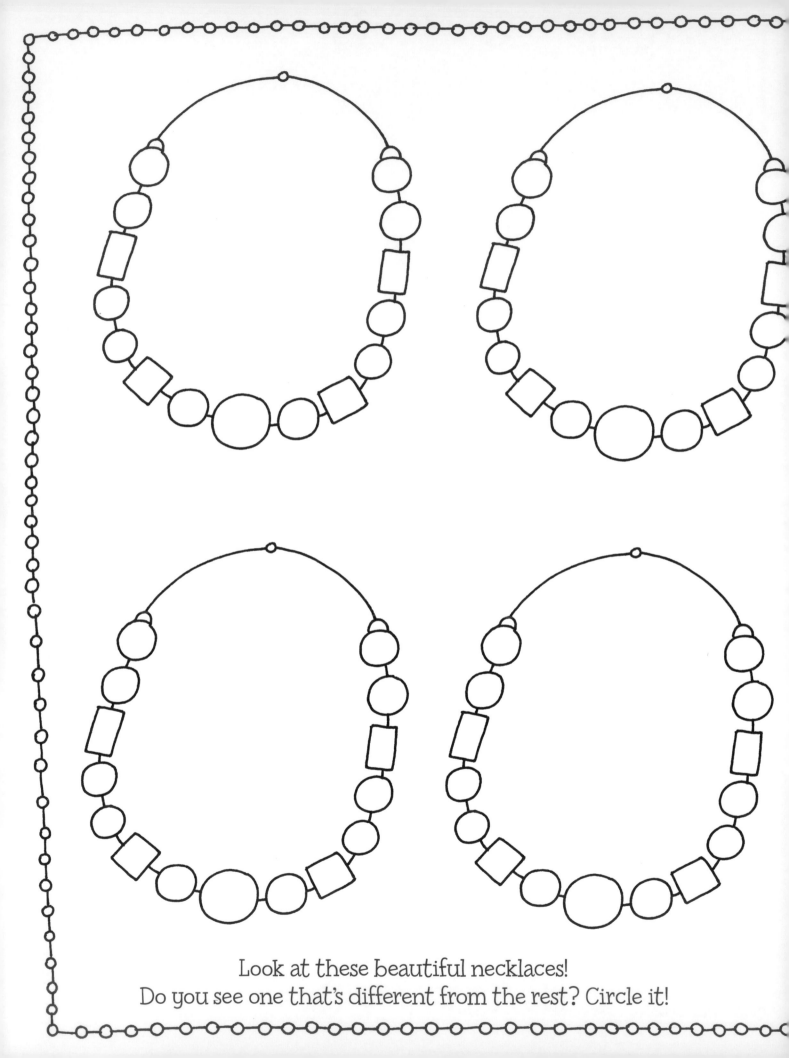

Look at these beautiful necklaces!
Do you see one that's different from the rest? Circle it!

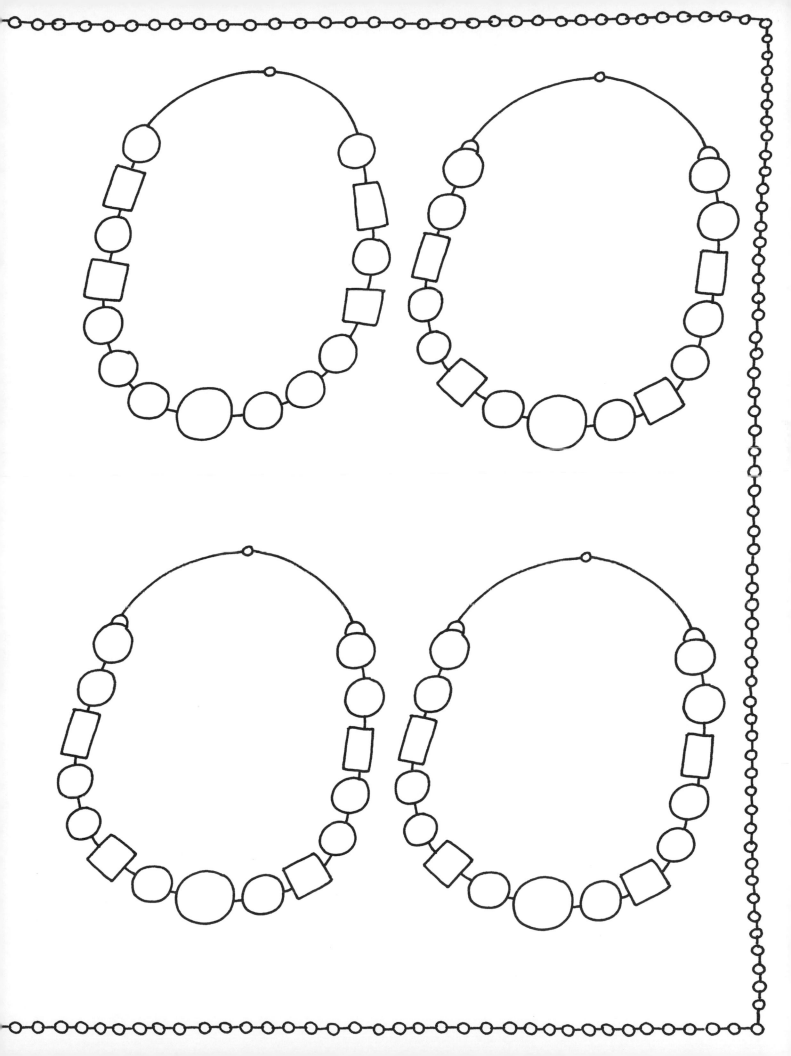

A little girl has lost her ring.
Can you help her find it?

Start

Finish

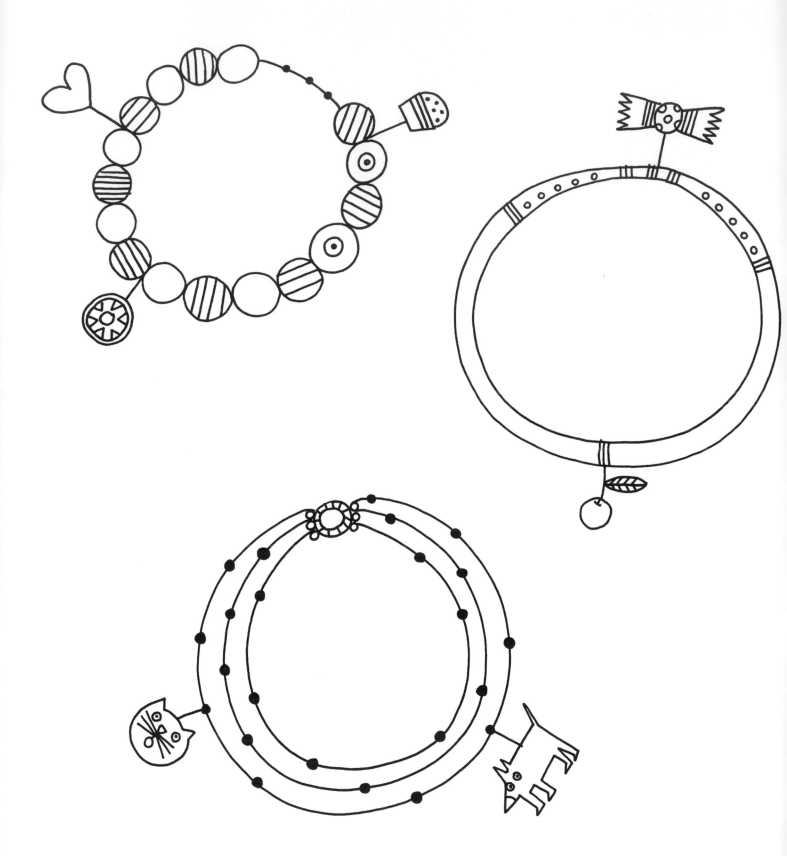

What pretty charm bracelets!
Can you add some more charms to them?

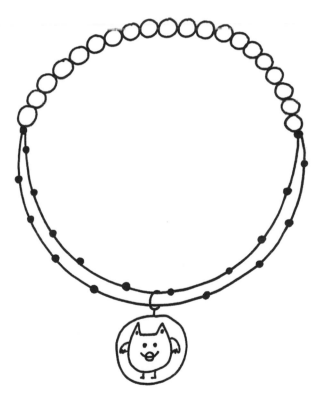

Draw some fun hats onto these ladies' heads.

These girls want to be ballerinas.
Can you give them some tutus?

Now color in the scene!

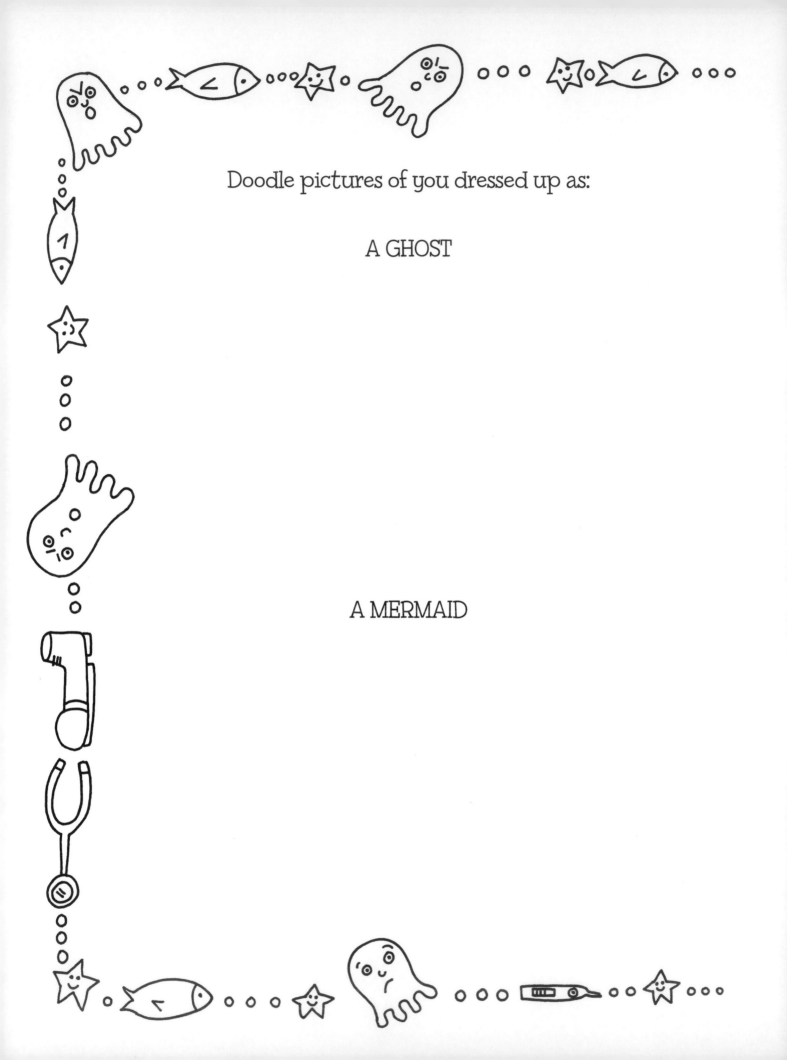

Doodle pictures of you dressed up as:

A GHOST

A MERMAID

A CLOWN

A DOCTOR

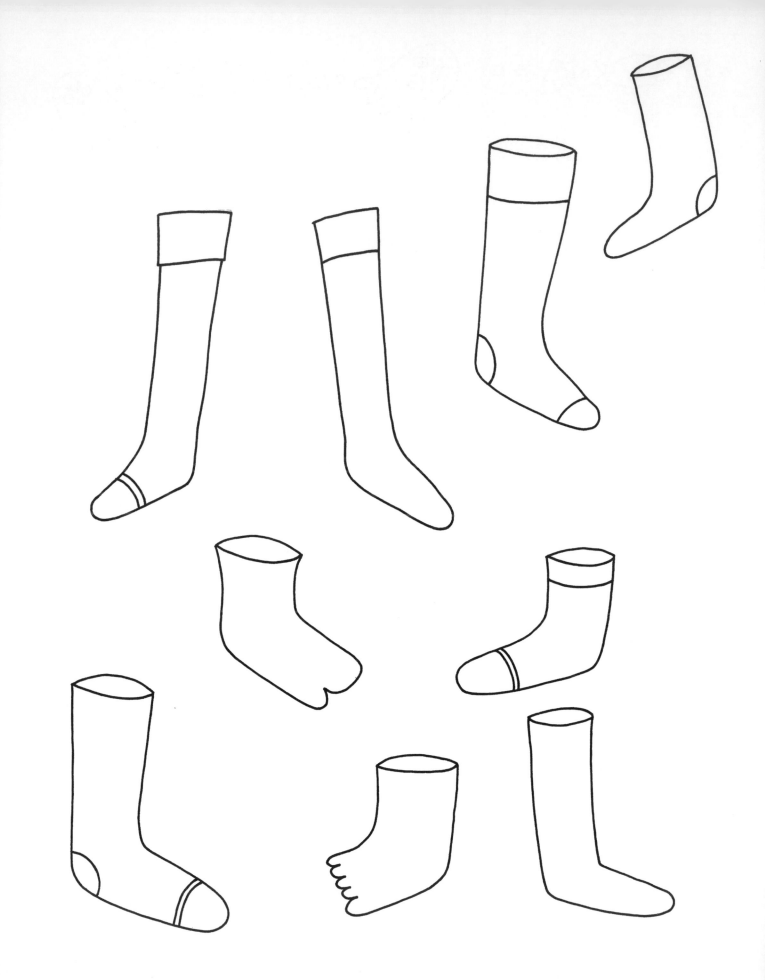

Decorate these socks with your favorite patterns!

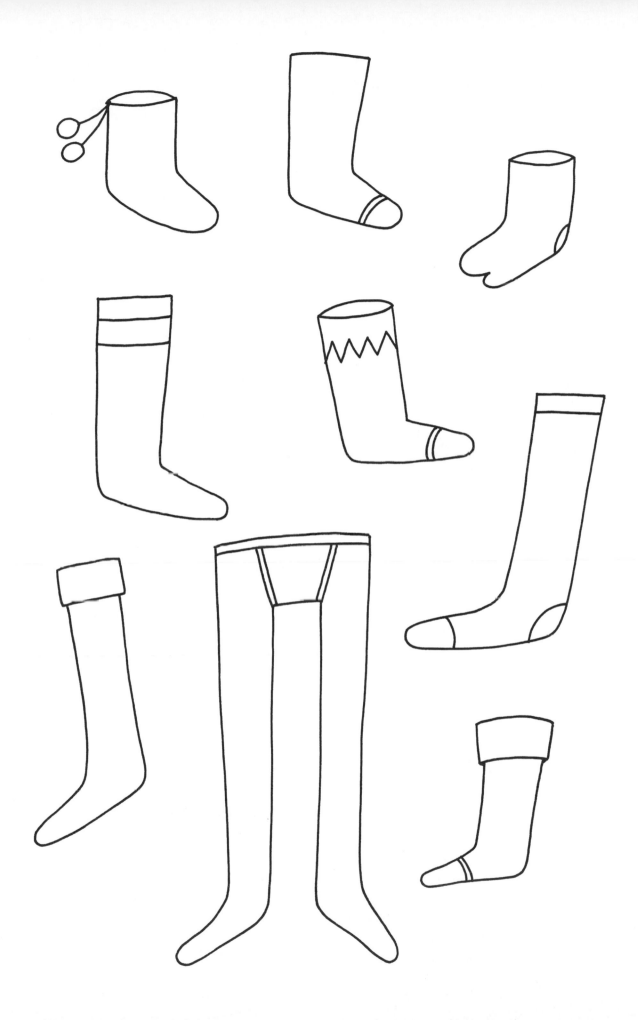

These kids have dressed up as pastry chefs.
Decorate their aprons any way you like!

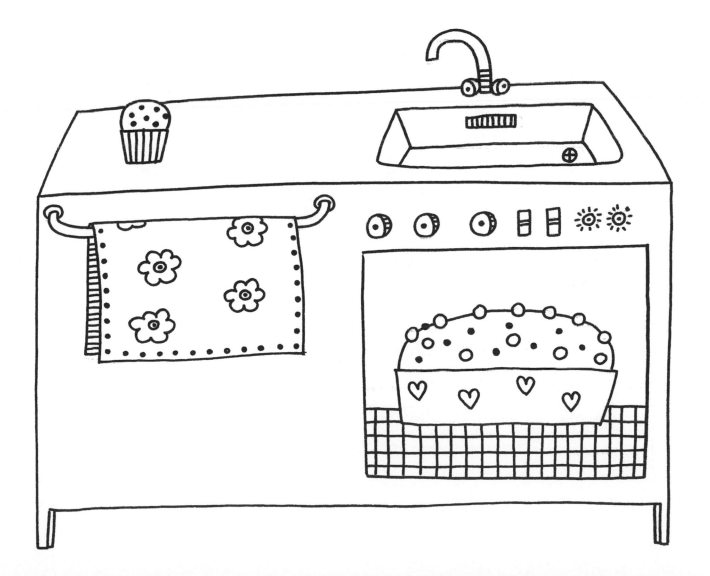

This cowboy and cowgirl can't find their hats.
Can you doodle some on them?

Now color in the scene!

Can you spot these images?
Color them in!

Color in these paper dolls any way you like!

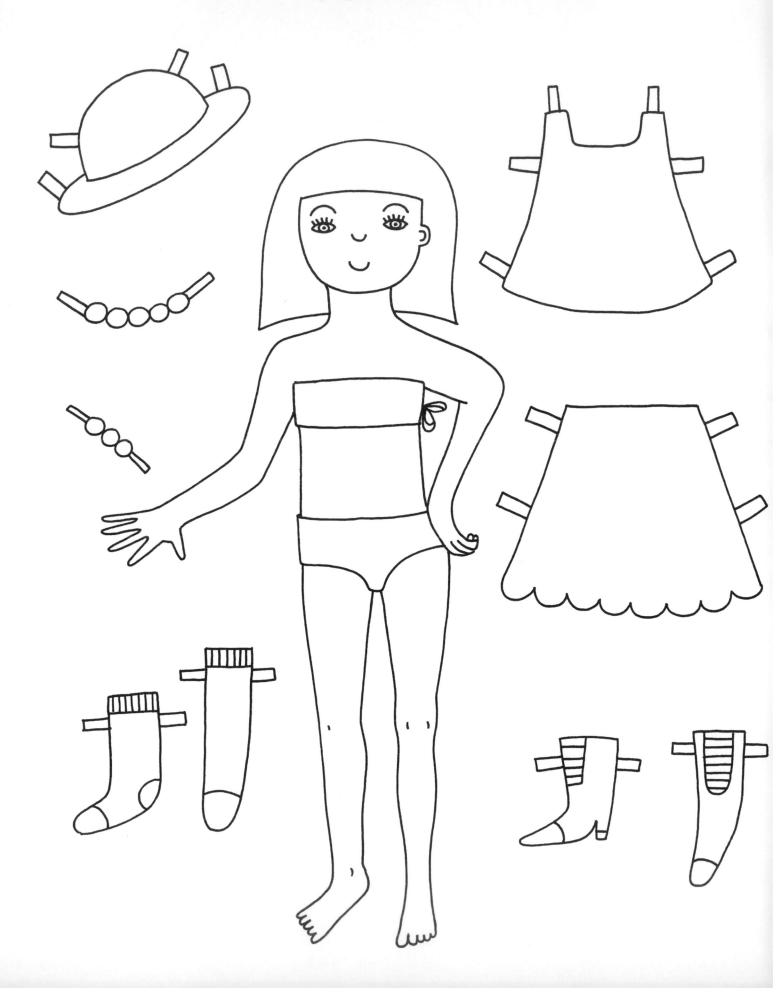

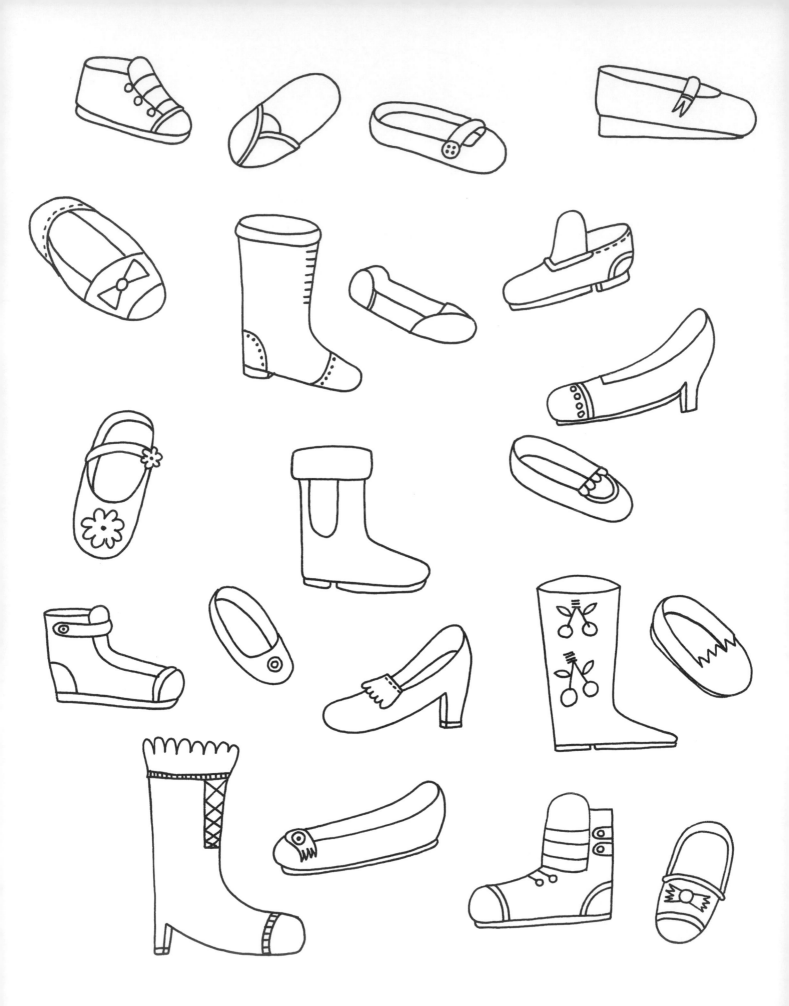

Can you find the six hats that look exactly like this one?
Circle them, and then color them in!

Yikes—a dragon!
Trace the dotted lines to create a knight that will scare it away!

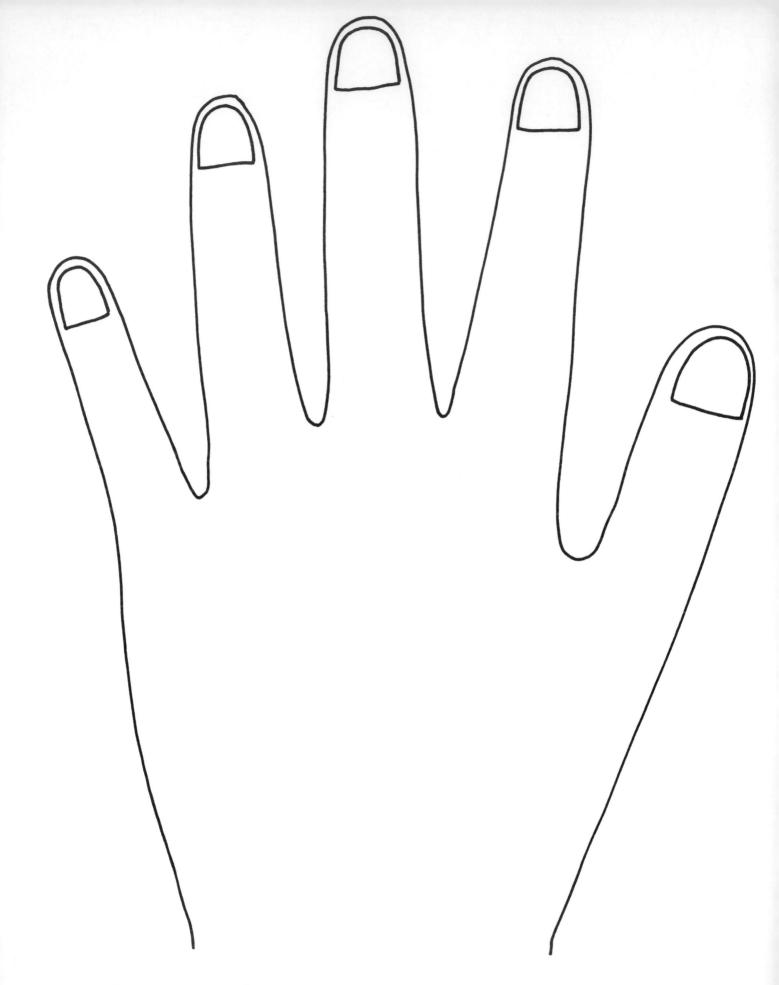

Decorate the fingernails on these hands any way you like!

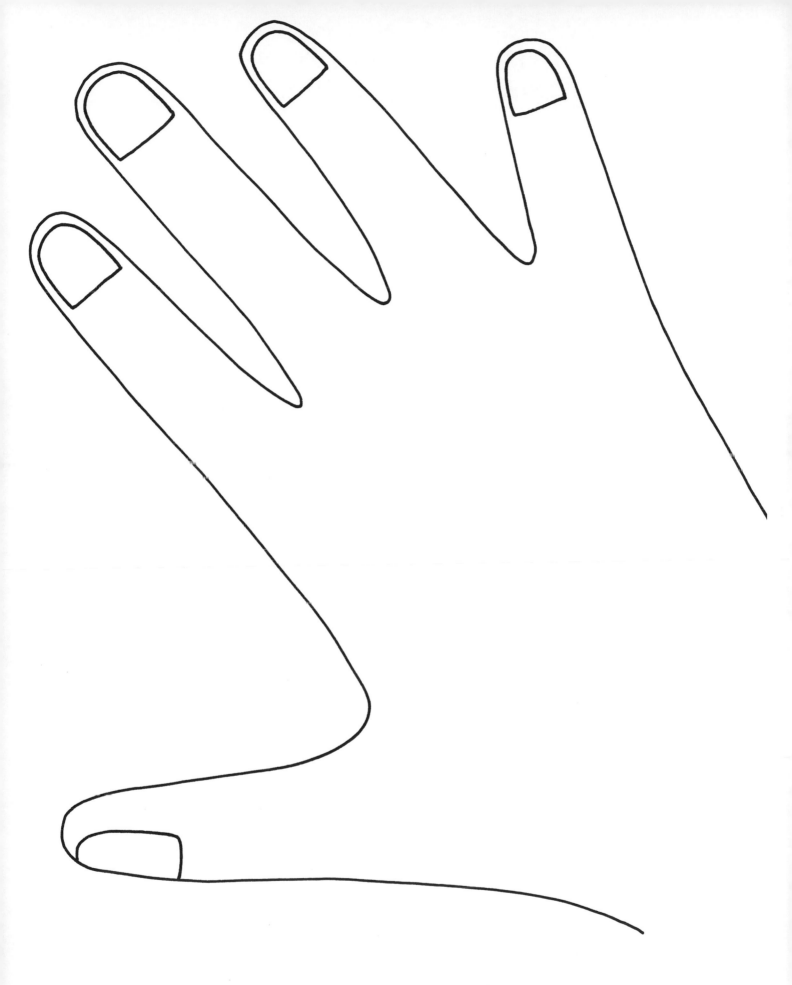

Then draw some rings on them!

This princess has lost her glass slipper!
Help her find it—and her prince!

Start

Finish

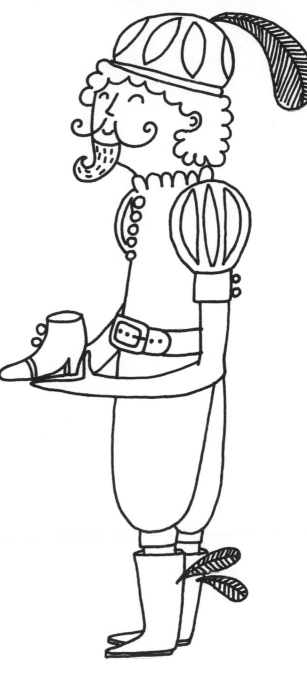

These kids want to go outside and play in the snow.
What clothes should they wear? Color them in!